ALL AROUND THE WORLD
UNITED ARAB EMIRATES

by Kristine Spanier, MLIS

pogo

Ideas for Parents and Teachers

Pogo Books let children practice reading informational text while introducing them to nonfiction features such as headings, labels, sidebars, maps, and diagrams, as well as a table of contents, glossary, and index.

Carefully leveled text with a strong photo match offers early fluent readers the support they need to succeed.

Before Reading

- "Walk" through the book and point out the various nonfiction features. Ask the student what purpose each feature serves.
- Look at the glossary together. Read and discuss the words.

Read the Book

- Have the child read the book independently.
- Invite him or her to list questions that arise from reading.

After Reading

- Discuss the child's questions. Talk about how he or she might find answers to those questions.
- Prompt the child to think more. Ask: What did you know about the United Arab Emirates before you read this book? What more would you like to learn?

Pogo Books are published by Jump!
5357 Penn Avenue South
Minneapolis, MN 55419
www.jumplibrary.com

Library of Congress Cataloging-in-Publication Data

Names: Spanier, Kristine, author.
Title: United Arab Emirates / Kristine Spanier.
Description: Minneapolis, MN: Jump!, Inc., 2022.
Series: All around the world
Includes index. | Audience: Ages 7-10
Identifiers: LCCN 2020058561 (print)
LCCN 2020058562 (ebook)
ISBN 9781636900278 (hardcover)
ISBN 9781636900285 (paperback)
ISBN 9781636900292 (ebook)
Subjects: LCSH: United Arab Emirates—Juvenile literature.
United Arab Emirates—Social life and customs—
Juvenile literature.
Classification: LCC DS247.T8 S68 2022 (print)
LCC DS247.T8 (ebook) | DDC 953.57—dc23
LC record available at https://lccn.loc.gov/2020058561
LC ebook record available at https://lccn.loc.gov/2020058562

Editor: Jenna Gleisner
Designer: Molly Ballanger

Photo Credits: Rasto SK/Shutterstock, cover; S-F/Shutterstock, 1; Pixfiction/Shutterstock, 3; Tomasz Czajkowski/Shutterstock, 4; Delstudio/Dreamstime, 5; Mahmoud Ghazal/Shutterstock, 6-7; trabantos/Shutterstock, 8-9; vivek gawade/Shutterstock, 10; David Steele/Shutterstock, 11; Dan Shachar/Shutterstock, 12-13tl; SeraphP/Shutterstock, 12-13tr; Sebastian Kennerknecht/SuperStock, 12-13bl; slowmotiongli/Shutterstock, 12-13br; Jiri Hera/Shutterstock, 14l; Kravtzov/Shutterstock, 14m; MShev/Shutterstock, 14r; Kdonmuang/Shutterstock, 15; Alexey Stiop/Shutterstock, 16-17; M7kk/Shutterstock, 18-19; Philip Lange/Shutterstock, 20-21; Henning Marquardt/Shutterstock, 23.

Printed in the United States of America at Corporate Graphics in North Mankato, Minnesota.

TABLE OF CONTENTS

CHAPTER 1

SEVEN EMIRATES

Burj Khalifa is the tallest building in the world. It is 2,716 feet (828 meters) high! It is in Dubai. Welcome to the United Arab Emirates (UAE)!

Burj Khalifa

The Palm Islands are off the coast of Dubai. These islands are **artificial**. They provide more land and beaches.

Abu Dhabi

Abu Dhabi is the **capital** of the UAE. This country is a **federation** in the Middle East. It is a group of seven **emirates**. Each emirate has a ruler. They are called **emirs**. They vote for a president. That leader is head of state. The president chooses a prime minister. This person leads the government.

TAKE A LOOK!

What are the seven emirates? Take a look!

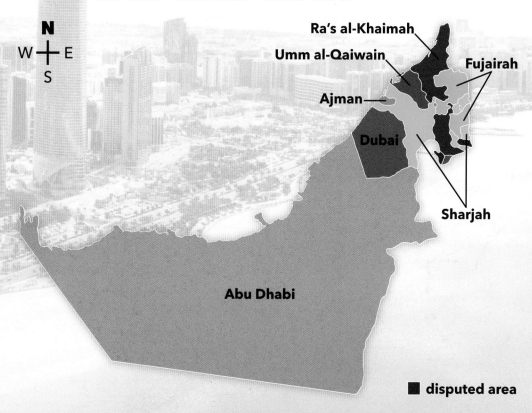

- Ra's al-Khaimah
- Umm al-Qaiwain
- Ajman
- Dubai
- Fujairah
- Sharjah
- Abu Dhabi

■ disputed area

Ajman is the smallest emirate. It is only 100 square miles (259 square kilometers). The Ajman **Fort** was built here around 1775. It was once the home of the emir. It is now a museum.

WHAT DO YOU THINK?

Most people who live in the UAE moved here from other countries. Many came here to work in oil jobs. Has your family moved? Why? How far did you move?

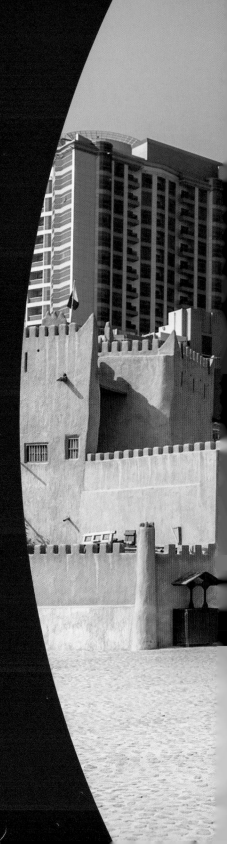

Ajman Fort

CHAPTER 2
LAND AND ANIMALS

Flamingos and many other birds **migrate** here. Why? The north coast is warm. There is a lot of food for them to eat.

The Rub' al Khali Desert covers much of the country. The **climate** is hot and dry. It can be 120 degrees Fahrenheit (49 degrees Celsius). It often rains less than six inches (15 centimeters) a year.

Red foxes and Arabian oryx live in the desert. Caracals live in rocky, wooded areas. Vultures fly the skies. They fly higher than 36,000 feet (10,973 m)! They **scavenge** for food.

WHAT DO YOU THINK?

The falcon is a **symbol** of strength and beauty. It is on **currency** here. Does your country's currency have symbols? What are they? What do they stand for?

red fox

Arabian oryx

caracal

vulture

CHAPTER 3

LIFE IN THE UAE

Fresh dates and figs grow here. People also eat kabsa. This is rice with meat or fish. Tabbouleh is a salad. Parsley, onion, and lemon juice flavor it.

tabbouleh

fig

kabsa

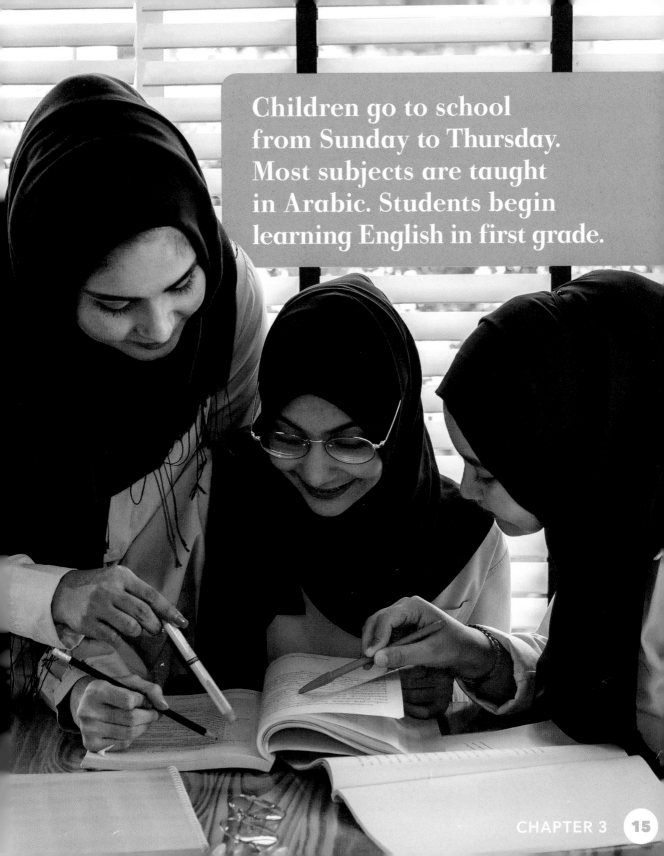

Children go to school from Sunday to Thursday. Most subjects are taught in Arabic. Students begin learning English in first grade.

More than half the **population** is **Muslim**. People visit **mosques** on Fridays. The Grand Mosque is in Abu Dhabi. People on the street can hear a call to prayer. It happens five times a day.

DID YOU KNOW?

It took 12 years to build the Grand Mosque. It has 82 domes. More than 40,000 people can fit inside at one time.

Grand Mosque

Sheep wool is dyed different colors. It is woven into colorful blankets and rugs. Camels and horses sometimes wear the blankets.

Many people watch camel races. Robots ride the camels instead of people! Jujitsu is popular here. This is a form of martial arts. Soccer is also popular.

There is much to see in the UAE. Do you want to visit?

robot

QUICK FACTS & TOOLS

UNITED ARAB EMIRATES

Location: Middle East

Size: 32,278 square miles
(83,600 square kilometers)

Population: 9,992,083
(July 2020 estimate)

Capital: Abu Dhabi

Type of Government:
federation of monarchies

Languages: Arabic, English,
Hindi, Malayalam, Urdu, Pashto,
Tagalog, Persian

Exports: crude oil, natural gas,
dried fish, dates

Currency:
United Arab Emirates dirham

artificial: Made by people rather than existing in nature.

capital: A city where government leaders meet.

climate: The weather typical of a certain place over a long period of time.

currency: The form of money used in a country.

emirates: States or countries of emirs.

emirs: Rulers, chiefs, or commanders in Islamic countries.

federation: A union of states, nations, or other groups joined together by an agreement.

fort: A place that is fortified against attack.

migrate: To move from one region or habitat to another.

mosques: Buildings where Muslims worship.

Muslim: People whose religion is Islam.

population: The total number of people who live in a place.

scavenge: To search for dead food to eat.

symbol: An object or design that stands for, suggests, or represents something else.

UAE's currency

INDEX

TO LEARN MORE

Finding more information is as easy as 1, 2, 3.

1 Go to www.factsurfer.com

2 Enter "UnitedArabEmirates" into the search box.

3 Choose your book to see a list of websites.

FACT SURFER